NATSUMI!

SUSAN LENDROTH • ILLUSTRATED BY PRISCILLA BURRIS

G. P. PUTNAM'S SONS

G. P. PUTNAM'S SONS

an imprint of Penguin Random House LLC
375 Hudson Street
New York, NY 10014

Library of Congress Cataloging-in-Publication Data
Names: Lendroth, Susan, author. | Burris, Priscilla, illustrator.
Title: Natsumi! / Susan Lendroth ; illustrated by Priscilla Burris.
Description: New York, NY : G. P. Putnam's Sons, 2018.
Summary: The festival of traditional Japanese arts is coming up, and little Natsumi's big personality is
too much for her family's quieter traditions, until her grandfather introduces her to taiko drumming.
Identifiers: LCCN 2016017387 | ISBN 9780399170904
Subjects: | CYAC: Festivals—Fiction. | Japan—Fiction.
Classification: LCC PZ7.L5384 Nat 2018 | DDC [E]—dc23
LC record available at https://lccn.loc.gov/2016017387

Manufactured in China by RR Donnelley Asia Printing Solutions Ltd.
ISBN 9780399170904
1 3 5 7 9 10 8 6 4 2

Design by Jaclyn Reyes.
Text set in Highlander ITC Std and Stoclet ITC Std.
The illustrations were created with digital brushes and pencils, found textiles, and paper.

To my one and only Pook.
—S.L.

For Mary, Debbie, and Kelly,
with admiration and gratefulness.

Thank you to Tony Sahara
and Shimpei Shirafuji.

—P.B.

For a small girl, Natsumi did everything in a big way.

She jumped high, played hard, and slurped noodles like a sumo wrestler. But . . .

"Not so *fast*, Natsumi!"
scolded Grandmother
when they went to the park.

"Not so *hard*, Natsumi!"
warned Father when she practiced
her ninja moves.

"Not so *loud*, Natsumi!"
called Mother every time
her daughter shut a door.

Only Grandfather smiled
and said nothing.

Each year, Natsumi's village held a festival of traditional Japanese arts, and her family spent weeks practicing for it. Natsumi wanted to try everything.

First, she gathered flowers with Grandmother, who carefully selected each bloom. Natsumi picked EVERYTHING.

"Let's shake out any bugs," said Grandmother. Tap, tap, tap—
she gently rapped the stems against her cupped palm. "Like this."

SLAP, SLAP, SLAP! Natsumi whipped her bouquet into a cloud
of pollen, leaves, and ants.

"Not so fast, Na-Na-NATSU-mi!" sneezed Grandmother.

In the afternoon, Father asked,
"Would you like to help me with
the tea ceremony?"

"**YES!**" Natsumi cried,
plopping down beside him.

Father measured powdered
tea into a bowl, poured hot
water, and carefully whisked
the mixture into froth the
color of spring grass.

Then he added tea and water to the second bowl and handed Natsumi the whisk.

She stirred;

she beat;

she whirled
her tea into
a cyclone.

Father wiped green flecks from his glasses.
"Not so hard, Natsumi," he said.

Later, Natsumi joined Mother at dance rehearsal. Girls and women dipped and turned, flicking fans open and shut like butterflies.

Natsumi flicked her fan open.
Then shut.

Open. **Whisht.** Shut. **Click.**

The harder she flicked,
the louder it snapped.
WHIISSHHHT! CLICK! WHIISSHHHT! CLICK!

She was a
samurai leading
troops to battle with
her mighty war fan.
Natsumi flung her
arms wide.

"YAAAHHH!"

Launched like a rocket, the fan twirled across the room
and bounced off Mrs. Tanaka's knee.

"Sorry!"
called Natsumi.

"Not so loud, Natsumi,"
whispered Mother.

That evening, Grandfather found her slumped outside. "Come, walk with me, Natsumi-chan," said Grandfather.

"No matter what I do, something always goes wrong," said Natsumi.
"I'm sure you'll find the right fit if you keep looking . . . and listening," replied Grandfather.

They strolled toward the village hall.
Natsumi heard a sound like muffled thunder.

BOOM!
Boom-boom. BOOM!

The very air seemed to quiver.

"Come on,
Grandfather,"
Natsumi urged.

For the next two weeks,
Grandfather met Natsumi after
school every day and brought
her home late each afternoon.

When Mother asked where they had been,
Natsumi replied, "It's a surprise."

On festival day, Grandmother's flowers brightened the stage,
Father served tea to the mayor, and Mother danced.

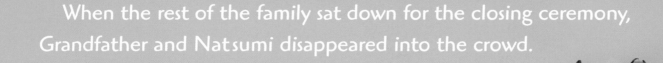

When the rest of the family sat down for the closing ceremony,
Grandfather and Natsumi disappeared into the crowd.

"Thank you for joining our celebration," said the mayor.

"Now we have one final performance, the beginning of
a new tradition for our village—our own taiko drummers!"

BOOM! Drumbeats shook the eaves.
BOOM! Grandmother felt her sandals vibrate.
BOOM! Boom-boom. BOOM! Boom-boom. BOOM!

"Look!" Father pointed at the smallest drummer on the stage. "Natsumi!"

BOOM! Boom-boom.
BOOM! Boom-boom.
BOOM! Boom-boom.

With each beat, Natsumi's sticks flew faster.
With each **BOOM**, she pounded harder.

And one day, Natsumi hoped to be the loudest drummer of them all.